The year is 1144 and the world's last dragon
has returned. The evil Lord ~~~~~~~~~~~~ ns to
us~~~~~~~~~~~~~~~~~~ rule the kingdom. Ac~~rding
to prophecy, only one person can stop him. And
that one person is a 16-year-old boy.

BOOK 1: *The Last Dragon* Jacob, Orson and Lia must
rescue the only egg of the world's last dragon.

BOOK 2: *A Hero's Worth* While the young dragon
grows, Lia may be forced to marry Lord Manning.

BOOK 3: *Draco's Fire* The fully grown dragon helps
Jacob fulfill the prophecy — and rescue his kingdom.

For my father, who passed on his love of fantasy books.

The DRAGON SPEAKER Series

Draco's Fire

E.L. THOMAS

LIBRARY AND ARCHIVES CANADA CATALOGUING IN PUBLICATION

Thomas E. L. (Erin L.)
    Draco's fire / E.L. Thomas.

(HIP fantasy)
(Dragon speaker ; 3)
ISBN 978-1-897039-48-9

I. Title. II. Series: HIP fantasy III. Series: Dragon speaker ; 3
PS8639.H572D73 2009   jC813'.6   C2009-903747-5

General editor: Paul Kropp
Text design: Laura Brady
Illustrations drawn by: Charlie Hnatiuk
Cover design: Robert Corrigan

1 2 3 4 5 6 7   13 12 11 10 09

Printed and bound in Canada

High Interest Publishing acknowledges the financial support of the Government of Canada through the Book Publishing Industry Development Program (BPIDP) for our publishing activities.

CONTENTS

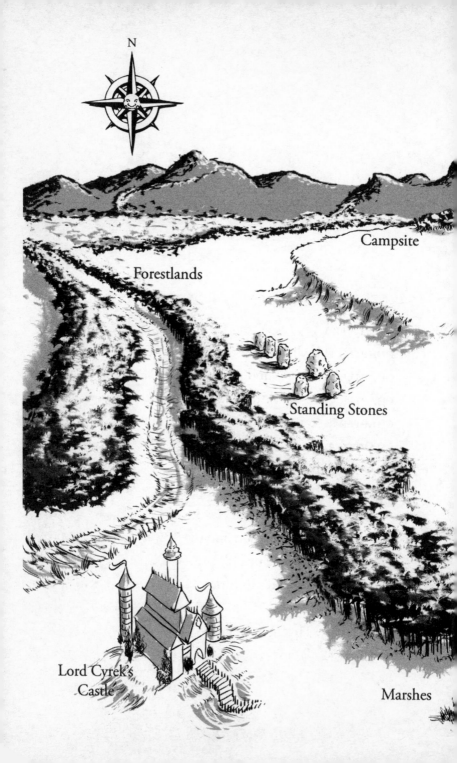

Claw Mountain

Mound Meadow

Farmlands

Lord Manning's Castle

Pine Abbey

Market Town

Great Forest

Village of Maldon

Previously

Dark times have fallen on the land of Kalmar. Lord Manning and the evil wizard Kain have seized power. They have killed any villagers who stood against them. They have hunted dragons nearly to extinction, killing them to steal their power.

A prophecy says that the Chosen One will restore the kingdom.

In Book One, *The Last Dragon*, Jacob and his friend Orson learn that one female dragon is still alive. The dragon's egg is being held by Lord Manning. Jacob, who has the power to hear and speak with birds, is told that he is the Chosen One. His friend Orson joins with him in a quest to take the dragon's egg from Lord Manning's castle. Soon they are joined by Lia, an elf who has been trained as a dragon healer. After much struggle, the three rescue the egg … and the baby dragon is born.

In Book Two, *A Hero's Worth*, Lia is caught by her father, the King of the Elves. The old man tells Lia that she must marry Lord Manning. Jacob and Orson vow to rescue her. The baby dragon is left with Aldous, a healer, and the two young men head off to Lord Manning's castle. Using their skills, their wits and the power of the young dragon, they rescue Lia. In the process, Jacob steals a magical white stone from Kain. Aldous tells him there is a second stone that he must find before he can fulfill the prophecy.

Now in Book Three, *Draco's Fire*, the dragon is fully grown. Jacob, Orson, Lia and the dragon have spent months in hiding and in training. At last they are ready to defeat Lord Manning and his wizard.

CHAPTER ONE | **Hiding Places**

Outside the cave, a blizzard raged.

Jacob blew on his fingers, trying to warm them, then tucked his hands under his armpits. "We'll freeze to death before we find that miserable stone," he said. The air was so cold it hurt to breathe. It felt much more like February than early April. That's what they got for climbing the highest mountain in Kalmar.

"We'll make it. We've made it this far," his friend Orson said. "Jacob, you're the Chosen One. You're the Dragon Speaker that will save the kingdom. A little snowstorm isn't going to stop you." He added another piece of wood to the small pile in the middle of the cave. This was all the firewood they had left.

Jacob grunted. This little snowstorm had nearly knocked their small group off Claw Mountain with its brutal winds. It had blinded them with snow and sent them rushing for shelter.

Chosen One. Chosen for what? To die, fighting a battle he couldn't win? Lord Manning had an entire army at his command. His wizard Kain had powerful magic and had already killed Jacob's family.

"Hey, we'll be fine," Orson told his friend. "You saved a dragon, remember? Surely you can find a little chunk of stone."

"Orson's right," Lia said, sitting down beside Jacob. "You have to find the dark half of the comet stone." She sounded tired. Her elf blood kept her warm, but she had used up a lot of energy healing Aldous.

The old man didn't belong on this mountain.

None of them did.

It had been a long year of hiding from Lord Manning and searching for the comet stone. There were months of training with Draco, the dragon. Months of searching for food and new places to hide while they barely stayed ahead of Lord Manning's guards. They all needed a rest.

"Is Aldous all right?" Jacob asked.

"For now," Lia said. "He's sleeping. At his age … his cough doesn't sound good."

"I can light the fire now," Orson said, glancing at the cave entrance. They were cold, but they couldn't risk having Lord Manning's men see their campfire.

"No one will see us with that storm blowing," Jacob said. He didn't want to admit how badly he wanted that fire, how much the thought of heat and light cheered him.

Jacob sighed and let his head fall forward. He heard the sound of flint striking stone, then the fire caught.

"How are you holding up?" Lia asked, leaning closer to him. "How's your leg?"

"It's fine," Jacob said shortly. If he admitted that his bad leg hurt, she'd want to look at it. Jacob hated the way his leg looked — scrawny and covered with scars.

Lia didn't press him. "We're not far off course, you know," she said. "If the storm clears, we'll reach the mountaintop tomorrow."

Jacob nodded. He pulled a stone from the pouch around his neck. It was pale white, round at one end, pointed and curved at the other — a little like a dragon's tooth. It had come from a comet that passed the Earth many years ago. Aldous said the stone had another half,

a dark half, and that the two together made a perfect circle. That was the stone he was searching for. Jacob needed them both if he was going to defeat Kain and Lord Manning.

And Jacob had just over two weeks to do it all. In a fortnight, the comet was coming back. Whatever Jacob was supposed to do, that was when he had to do it.

He closed his eyes, feeling the fire's warmth on his face.

"Jacob?" Lia's voice broke in on his thoughts. "Does it usually do that?"

"Do what?" His eyes snapped open. The light stone was glowing.

When he looked at it, it grew brighter, then faded.

Jacob knew that the light stone had power. It had saved Draco's life, once. But having worked so well that one time, the stone simply wouldn't work for him again. And for whatever reason, it didn't seem to work at all for Lia or Orson. Aldous refused to try.

Glowing, though. That was new.

"Jacob?" Orson's voice came from the back of the cave. "This isn't a cave. It's a tunnel."

Jacob turned to look where Orson was pointing. The cave narrowed at the back, but the two walls didn't quite meet. On impulse, Jacob held up the light stone.

The stone had guided them well over the winter months — when he held it in his fist, he knew which way to go. Aldous said the light stone would lead them to the other half of the stone, the dark half. And Jacob felt it now, the invisible pull, tugging him toward the tunnel.

"I'm going to see where it leads."

Jacob carried the stone in front of him, following its glow as he entered the dark tunnel. Orson fell in behind him. The tunnel grew smaller until Jacob had to crouch. He turned sideways to squeeze through the narrow parts.

"Jacob, I can't," Orson said, his voice strangely high. "I'm stuck."

Jacob turned to face his friend. It was true. The cave walls that pressed in on Jacob had trapped Orson.

"I don't like you going on alone," Orson said. "Wait, I'll get Lia."

But Jacob needed to keep going. He couldn't explain it. "I'll be safe," he said. "I just … this can't wait." The stone was hot in his hand.

Orson looked at him for a long moment. Jacob gave what he hoped was a smile, then turned his back on Orson and set off.

The tunnel grew narrower before it got wider again. For once, Jacob was glad of his small size. In the dark, it was hard to tell how long he had been walking. An hour, maybe more? A narrow, frozen stream crossed the tunnel floor like a ribbon. The glow from the stone glittered on the ice.

Keeping his hand nearby, Jacob set the comet stone down on the ice. The comet stone swung around so the sharp end was pointing along the tunnel. He was headed the right way, then.

But he had known that, already. He felt it in his gut. The stone wanted him to continue this way, wanted him to hurry.

As Jacob walked on, the air became fresher. The tunnel angled up, toward the surface. A hint of light ahead lured him on.

Finally, Jacob arrived. A narrow opening, barely tall enough to crawl through, led out of the tunnel. He got down on all fours and looked. It seemed to lead to a clearing, but snow and a large boulder blocked his view. He started to make his way around it but stopped when he heard voices.

"The General thinks the storm did 'em in," a man said. "An old man and three brats. No reason we should still be up here, freezing like this."

Jacob held his breath and ducked back into the tunnel. He stuffed the glowing stone back into the leather pouch around his neck.

Another man snorted. "Kain won't let us off the mountain until we show him their dead bodies," he said. "Besides, did you forget about the stone?"

Kain. Jacob pressed his tongue into the space where a tooth had been. The wizard took a tooth from each of his victims before he killed them. Then Kain wore them knotted into his hair. One of those trophy teeth had been Jacob's. But Jacob had survived.

Jacob leaned as close to the entrance as he dared, straining to see without being seen. Peering past the boulder, he spotted two of Lord Manning's guards.

"Bloody nonsense if you ask me," the first guard said. "Got half the palace guard up here looking for a rock on a mountaintop. He wants a rock? I'll give him a rock." The guard scooped up a fist-sized stone and hurled it. It bounced off the boulder in front of Jacob and rolled into the tunnel, narrowly missing Jacob's foot.

"Huh. That's strange," the guard said. "It should have bounced back." Slowly he approached Jacob's hiding place.

CHAPTER TWO
Dreams and Prophecies

Jacob pressed himself into the dark shadows.

"Rabbit hole," the guard called. "Wanna see if there's anything in it?"

"Forget it. Let's just get back. It's too cold out here," the second guard said.

Jacob waited until they were long gone before he risked moving.

When Jacob got back to the cave, Aldous, Lia and Orson were eating. The smell of fried mushrooms filled the air.

"We saved you some," Orson said, poking the pan with his foot. "There's a bit of that dried rabbit meat, too."

While he ate, Jacob told them what he had found. "I think that's where the stone wants me to go," he said. "It was glowing. It's hard to explain, but I felt like I was supposed to go out there."

"But if what you said is true, Lord Manning's men are patrolling the whole area," Orson said. "There's no way we'll get past them."

Lia's eyes narrowed. "I'd like to try," she said. She placed one hand on her bow. Lia had her own reasons to hate Lord Manning — the man her father wanted her to marry.

"No one doubts your skill with an arrow," Aldous said. "And yet, even an elf may find it difficult to take on an army." His voice was kind, but firm.

Lia scowled.

"What do we do?" Jacob asked Aldous.

"Do? Very little, at the moment," the old man said. "The stone will be found when the time is right. Depend on it." He turned to Jacob. "For now, you might want to warn Draco to stay far away. If Kain is nearby, he is in danger."

Kain had killed Draco's mother and hunted nearly all

the dragons to their deaths. Draco was the last male dragon. His mother had told Jacob that, before she died. If there were any female dragons left, they'd gone into hiding. And they were smart to stay there.

The wizard Kain got stronger every time he killed. The more powerful his prey, the stronger he got. The power Kain got from the death of a dragon was terrifying.

Because Jacob was a dragon speaker, he alone had the power to speak to Draco. Reaching with his mind, Jacob filled Draco in on all that had happened. For now, Draco was safely hidden from Lord Manning's men. If he came closer, there would be danger.

I don't like it, Draco thought.

Be careful, Jacob thought. *Stay close, but keep out of sight.*

In response, Draco sent him a rush of feelings — warmth and worry flooded through Jacob.

Jacob smiled. *Yeah. I'll be careful, too.*

Lia was watching him closely. "You're getting better at connecting with Draco," she said. "You don't even have to try any more, do you?"

Embarrassed, Jacob shook his head. The link he and Draco shared was so much a part of him now that he didn't think about it.

Aldous nodded. "The time you spend with Draco strengthens your bond," he said. "Soon you will need that strength."

"But why, Aldous?" Jacob asked, stepping forward. "We need to know the truth. It's time you told us how to fulfill the prophecy."

"The prophecy is unclear," Aldous told them. He gazed into the fire. "The first two verses, you know. Here is the last.

Two become one, or one shall fail:
The Chosen One's birthright.
That which was broken must be healed,
When fire burns the night."

And that made about as much sense as the other two verses — no sense at all. Was nothing ever simple? Jacob sighed.

Orson looked disappointed, too. "But what does it mean?"

Aldous sighed. "I can tell you only this. When the comet returns, the two stones must be brought together. That is your only hope of ever stopping Kain."

Lia looked up, startled. Jacob caught on a second later.

"*Your*. You said *your* only hope, not *our* only hope," Jacob said. "Why?"

But Aldous was already stretching out on his bedroll by the fire. "An old man gets tired," he said. He lay down and closed his eyes.

"Aldous," Jacob said softly.

Aldous's eyes snapped open. "I've lived a long time, Jacob. I feel it in my bones. This comet will be the end of me, one way or the other." His voice tapered off and he turned away. Then there was silence.

"I'll take first watch," Lia said.

So Jacob lay down by the fire and waited as Aldous's breath turned to wheezes and Orson's snore filled the cave. Jacob waited and waited for sleep that was a long time coming.

~

Jacob woke from a dream of falling. "No!" The word started in his dream and finished in his waking mind.

"Are you okay?" Orson asked.

Jacob nodded. The smell of the campfire mingled with wild mint. There was a weight on his chest. He looked down to see Lia's head resting on him, her hair tangled and spread about in sleep. He lay back. All the nights they had spent together hiding in the forest, she had never been this close to him before. He was almost afraid to breathe.

"Grab some more sleep if you can," Orson said. "I'm not tired." He yawned.

It wasn't the first time Orson had tried to take an extra watch so Jacob wouldn't have to. Jacob knew Orson meant well, but he could look after himself.

He was the Chosen One. It was his fault they were all here.

"I'm awake," Jacob said. He eased himself out from under Lia. His body felt cold where she had been pressed against him.

He walked to the cave entrance and peered out.

The blizzard was gone. Against the black night, stars sparkled like sunlight on water. They seemed so far away.

It made the prophecy hard to believe — what did stars and comets care about life on Earth?

"Thought I heard something earlier," Orson said. Jacob heard him moving in the cave, settling down to sleep. "Sounded like a bear."

Jacob felt a smile crease his face. "It would be something if he wanted to come in here, wouldn't it?" He wasn't sure why he found the idea funny. A bear was dangerous, but so … ordinary, after everything they'd been through. Dragons. Wizards. A prophecy.

"We'd handle it," Orson said. He yawned again. After a moment, his rumbling snore filled the cave again. Maybe the noise would keep the bears away.

Lost in thought, Jacob leaned against the cave wall. An owl flew past. Lazily, he greeted it.

"What does he say?" Lia asked from behind him.

Jacob jumped. "You scared me."

Lia sat beside him, gazing up at the sky through the narrow opening as the owl circled. "I wish I could hear the birds, the way you do. Draco, too. You have such an amazing gift."

Jacob didn't answer. It was a long time since he had thought of his mind speech that way. His gift was too tied in with all that had happened. All he had lost.

"Have you ever tried to make it so someone else can

hear?" Lia asked. "Sometimes when I heal, I get a glimpse of the other person's mind. Maybe if we both tried at the same time."

Jacob thought for a moment. It was such a private part of himself. Could he share it? He reached out with his mind. The owl was there, thinking only about her hunt and the shift of the wind under her wings.

"We can try," he said to Lia.

They joined hands. Lia's hands felt small, cool and fragile in his.

She closed her eyes and raised her chin. "I'm ready," she said. Her face was inches away, eyes closed, lips parted.

Jacob's palms grew sweaty. Did she notice?

"Jacob?" Lia asked.

Jacob cleared his throat. "Uh, yeah. I just need to focus." He closed his own eyes. He reached for Lia with his thoughts in the same way as he spoke to birds. He felt the connection snap into place. It was as if the owl's thoughts flowed through him into Lia.

Lia jerked back, her hands flying out of his. She screamed.

Startled, Jacob dropped the connection. "I'm sorry!" He knelt beside Lia.

Lia trembled as he helped her sit up. "You're bleeding," Jacob said.

Slowly, Lia touched a hand to her nose, staring when it came away bloody.

"Here," Jacob said. He tore off a corner of his shirt and handed it to her. "I'm sorry," he said again.

He should have known better. He remembered how painful it had been for him at first, before he learned to protect his mind.

He was an idiot. He'd been showing off, trying to impress Lia. He had hurt her.

Aldous rose up behind them. "Fools!" he said. "If you wanted to call Kain to us, you've done well." The old man ignored Jacob, kneeling instead beside Lia. He peered into her eyes. "No harm done, I think," he muttered. "You should be glad you're an elf."

Lia rubbed her head. "What did you mean, call Kain to us?"

Aldous glared. "Your scream would have woken the dead."

Jacob's face grew hot. "It's fine," he said. "I beat him once, I can do it again." The boast sounded empty even to him.

Aldous laughed. "Is that what you think? Because you had him at your mercy once? A dragon's tooth pressed against his guts? There are ways to get rid of the wizard. That is not one of them."

Orson, who had joined them, frowned. "Then why …?"

"Kain was taunting him," Aldous said. "Had Jacob struck down a helpless man, the light stone would never have answered to him."

"A knight shows mercy," Orson whispered.

Jacob's mind raced. "You said the light stone wouldn't have answered to me. What about the dark stone? Is it the same? If Lord Manning or Kain has to prove worthy, they probably won't be able to use it, right?"

"The dark stone will grant any heart's wish," Aldous sighed. There was a strange smile on his face. "But the stone will twist the wish so that the person regrets it forever."

Lia pulled the red-streaked cloth away from her nose. "The bleeding has stopped," she said.

"Why did the bird's voice hurt her?" Jacob asked.

Aldous glared at him. "Did you think yours was a common gift? Did you think any mind was able to handle it? Or did you not bother to think at all?"

Jacob looked at his feet.

"Quiet," Orson said. "Listen."

Jacob heard footsteps on snow.

CHAPTER THREE | Under Attack

They listened to the approaching footsteps.

"Ten men," Lia said. "No more than twelve."

"Maybe a scouting party," Jacob whispered. "They might not know we're here." He very much wanted to believe that.

Aldous pulled his mouth into a thin line. "We can't take that chance."

"Not a lot of choice, is there?" Jacob said.

Orson drew his sword and moved toward the cave's entrance. "Actually, there is," he said. "The tunnel."

25

"But — you can't get through," Jacob said.

"You can." Orson's face was deadly calm. He slashed his sword through the air, getting the balance. "I'll buy you time."

"No! Aldous, tell him no," Jacob said.

Outside, the footsteps grew louder. "Light ahead, sir," a voice said. "A campfire."

A look passed between Orson and Aldous. Jacob didn't like it.

"He's right," Aldous said. "You must find the dark stone, Jacob. At all costs."

A voice came from outside. "This might be a cave. I'm going in."

Jacob drew his sword.

"There's no time for this," Orson whispered. "Get Lia and Aldous to safety. Promise me." He stared at Jacob until Jacob nodded once, angrily.

Without another word, Jacob snatched a burning torch from the fire and handed it to Lia. He herded Lia and Aldous into the tunnel, praying that they'd be fast enough.

Jacob looked over his shoulder just as Orson thrust his sword through the face of the first guard.

Orson whirled, pulling his sword free. He spotted Jacob. "Run! Go!"

Jacob ran, chasing Aldous and Lia down the tunnel. Back they went, further and further from the main cave, slowing only when the tunnel grew narrow. But when Jacob heard the ring of steel on steel, he stopped.

"I can't," he said. He yanked off the pouch that contained the light stone, then threw it at Lia. "Sorry, Aldous. Lia, get him out of here. Find the other stone."

He turned and ran.

The cave was empty. Orson had taken the fight outside, making sure no guards slipped past him.

Draco! Jacob sent. *I need you!* He charged outside, grabbing his bow and arrows. Dawn was just starting to colour the sky.

The narrow ledge worked to Orson's advantage; the guards could come at him only one or two at a time. Jacob saw the body of the first guard Orson had killed, his blood staining the snow. Orson must have used him as a shield, to get out of the cave.

Orson's back was to Jacob. He was fighting two guards, moving so fast his sword blurred. With a twist of his sword, he sent one man flying off the ledge.

It was a long way down.

Orson was on one knee now, barely holding his own against a tall guard. Jacob fired an arrow through the guard's throat. The man dropped his sword, then toppled slowly off the cliff.

Orson stared at Jacob. "You shouldn't be here," he called, blocking the next guard's sword thrust. He forced himself to his feet.

"You're welcome," Jacob said, firing another arrow.

There were six men left. Six wasn't so many, not for the two of them.

Jacob aimed past Orson, at the crowd on the ledge. So he didn't see when Orson's opponent flung his sword. Didn't notice it wheeling through the air until it was nearly too late. Jacob dodged. The blade missed his head, but it sliced into his left shoulder.

He dropped his bow, his legs sliding out from under him.

Orson spun around, his eyes wide. "Jacob! No!"

Jacob watched Orson's sword swing, watched as first the guard's severed head fell, spraying blood, then the body. Everything seemed to move very slowly.

He tried to lift his arm. Nothing happened. He felt cold, very cold, everywhere but his shoulder. His shoulder burned.

Orson's face appeared in front of him. "Hold on," he said. His voice sounded far away. Then he disappeared. Jacob heard steel hitting steel, heard a man scream.

I'm coming, Jacob. Draco's voice echoed across his mind.

One arm. He couldn't shoot a bow with one arm. But he still had a sword.

He pulled himself to his feet, leaning against the cliff wall. The world swayed. Jacob held on, willed his mind to clear. He pulled his sword free and held it in front of him.

Five guards left. Five against two.

But as he thought that, Orson lost his sword, in a movement too fast for Jacob's eyes to follow. All he saw was the sword, flying end over end, flashing in the sunlight and disappearing down the cliff. Then Orson sank to his knees.

The guard facing Orson laughed. "Not so brave now," he said.

And then a shadow fell over them. Draco's shrill war cry blasted the air. It was the only warning the guards got. A stream of flame poured over the two guards at the rear. They died before they could even scream.

Good, Draco! Jacob thought.

But two other guards pulled out bows and shot large arrows at Draco as he wheeled around for another attack. Draco shrieked in anger and pain. The backlash through Jacob's mind nearly made him pass out.

"Jacob!" Orson shouted.

Jacob snapped his eyes open. There was something wrong. Arrows couldn't harm Draco. Except for the one weak spot under the dragon's neck, arrows couldn't penetrate his silver scales. So why …?

Rough hands grabbed him. "Magic arrows," the guard said, pulling Jacob in front of him like a shield. Another guard had done the same with Orson. "A gift from Kain. We don't have many, but it won't take that many, will it? Call your dragon off, unless you want more holes in him."

Draco, stay back! Jacob sent.

Draco beat his large wings to stay in place. *I'll kill the guard*, Draco thought. *Can you move away? A foot to your left and I can kill him.*

It's too dangerous, Jacob thought.

The last guard had his arrow trained on Draco. "If he comes an inch closer, I'll shoot," he yelled.

Draco turned toward him, hissing.

"No!" shouted the guard who held Jacob. He shoved Jacob, hard, off the cliff.

Jacob heard a scream. It was Draco's, not his own.

Then he was falling through space.

CHAPTER FOUR | Return to the Cave

Jacob fell. Wind scraped against his skin, shapes went blurring past him.

But quicker than a thought, Draco was there. Jacob opened his mouth to shout, but the dragon had already caught him. Draco's claws gripped Jacob's flesh, his wings sent a huge downdraft of air, and Jacob stopped falling.

The stop wrenched his whole body. He hung like a puppet from Draco's claws, staring at the rocks below, then darkness took him.

Jacob woke up on rough ground. Trees framed his view of the sky. The sun was high overhead. *What happened?*

Draco sent him an image of Orson being dragged away by the guards. *I couldn't stop them,* the dragon thought.

Jacob sat up. The movement sent a tearing pain through his shoulder. The blood had clotted, sticking his clothing to his skin.

Careful, you'll make it bleed again, Draco thought.

Too late. Jacob pressed his hand against the wound. It wasn't going to kill him, but he couldn't let it keep bleeding like this. *You're going to have to help me.*

Draco used his fire to heat Jacob's dagger. Jacob wrapped his shirt around his hand to protect it, then picked up the weapon and pressed the flat of the blade against his wound. It sizzled when it burned his skin and hurt more than the sword wound had.

The smell made his stomach lurch. He dropped the dagger, then threw up behind an oak tree.

I'm sorry, Draco thought.

Jacob's answering laugh sounded a little scary, even to him. He wiped his mouth, glad that he didn't have to speak. *I'll live,* Jacob thought. *Now help me get back up that mountain. I need to find Aldous and Lia.*

Draco carried him most of the way up the mountain, but Jacob still had to walk to the cave. The ledge that led there was too narrow for Draco to land. It was easier walking this time, with no blizzard. Still, by the time the cave came in sight, afternoon shadows were long.

Jacob had wondered if the cave would be guarded, but they saw no one.

Be careful, Draco thought, as Jacob approached the entrance. *They might be inside.*

Jacob drew his dagger, the only weapon he had left. No sound came from inside the cave.

He crouched down and crawled through the opening.

Strong hands grabbed him and pulled him into the dark. Jacob found himself pinned to the cave floor, cold steel against his neck.

"State your name or I slit your throat," a familiar voice growled.

"Orson?" Jacob asked.

There was a pause, then the knife was pulled away. "You're lucky I know your voice."

There was a cracking sound, stone against flint, then a torch flared up, lighting the cave.

Jacob lifted his head. "You're … how …? I saw them take you," he said. "How did you …"

Orson looked away. "I escaped," he said. He had a

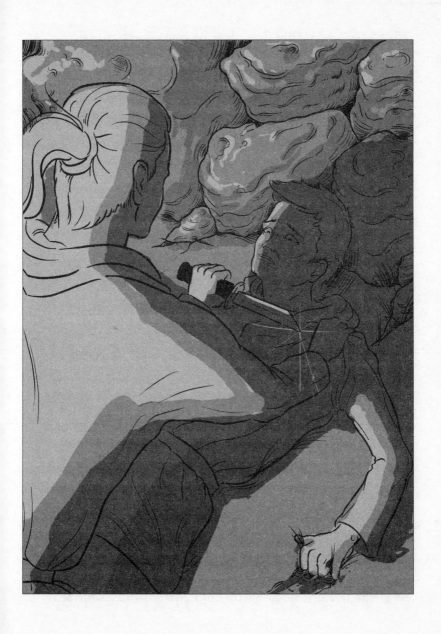

black eye, but other than that, he looked unharmed.

"How?" Jacob asked. He sat up, wincing at the pain in his shoulder.

"Long story," Orson said. "The important thing is, you're here. Now we can find the dark stone."

The stone! Where had it gone?

"I don't have it," Jacob said. "The light stone, I mean. I gave it to Lia. Where are Lia and Aldous?" It was strange that they hadn't returned to the cave. Had they escaped out the other end of the tunnel?

"You gave it to Lia?" Orson sounded shocked. "But they didn't find it on her."

"They? What do you mean, they?" Jacob asked. His lungs felt cold. He didn't trust his voice. "Lord Manning's men?"

Orson nodded.

Lord Manning's men had Lia.

Kain had Lia.

Jacob's hands curled into fists. "Tell me where," he said.

"Jacob, no," Orson said, grabbing his arms to keep him from standing. "You can't help if you get yourself killed."

This was a switch. Orson, the voice of reason?

"He'll hurt her," Jacob said. The words sounded

small, too small for what Kain might do. But it was all Jacob could bear to say.

No. Leaving Lia at Kain's mercy was impossible. He'd find a way to rescue her and Aldous, then he'd look for the stone.

Orson let go of Jacob's arms. "I hate it, too," he said. "But we don't have a choice. Think about it. Lord Manning and Kain are after these stones for a reason. Just you and I alone, even with Draco, we don't stand a chance against an army. But with those stones?" Orson paused, watching Jacob. "It's what Lia and Aldous would want you to do."

Jacob didn't like it, but Orson was right. There was only one problem. "Lia had the light stone," he said. "It's in Kain's hands, now. We won't ever find the dark stone without it."

Orson shook his head. "I told you, they didn't find it on her," he said. "She must have hidden it."

In the tunnels. It was the only place that made sense. But … "How do you know that?" Jacob asked. "How do you know they didn't find it on her?"

"I overheard," Orson said. But he didn't meet Jacob's eyes.

There was something wrong, something Orson didn't want Jacob to know. Was it shame? Shame that he had gotten away, but hadn't helped Lia and Aldous?

"You were that close to them?" Jacob asked, trying to picture what had happened.

"Yes!" Orson said. He glared at Jacob. "Yes, I was that close. And no, there was nothing I could do. Nothing! Do you want to keep talking about this, or do you want to find the stone?"

Jacob looked steadily at Orson.

"Sorry," Orson said. He opened his mouth like he was going to say more, but stopped. He kicked a rock so hard that it broke against the cave wall.

Then Jacob understood. The way he felt about Lia — Orson felt the same way. The fact that he hadn't saved Lia was eating him up inside.

"I'll check the tunnel," Jacob said.

CHAPTER FIVE | The Dark Stone

Jacob made his way through the tunnel. It was slow going, with one arm injured and the other holding a torch. The first trip had been so much easier — the rock bright and glowing in his fist, drawing him onwards.

Now, with each step he took, he looked all around. Lia could have hidden the stone anywhere. He didn't even know for sure that it was in the tunnel, but where else could it be?

He reached the place where the thin, frozen stream wound through the ground.

Lia and Aldous had been well hidden, here. Few of Lord Manning's men were small enough to come in after them. Jacob bent down, brushing his fingers over the ice. Here was water for drinking. They could have lasted for days.

If Lia had hidden the stone, it meant she had known she was headed into danger. If she had known that, why not just stay in the tunnel? He badly needed to talk to someone about all this.

Draco? he sent. Moments later he felt the mind of the dragon. He told the dragon all that had happened. *It seems unlikely that Lord Manning just happened to send his smallest guards.*

Unless he knew where Lia and Aldous were hiding, Draco thought.

Jacob hesitated. *But the only way he could know is …* He let the thought trail off.

Jacob had figured Orson was upset that he hadn't been able to rescue Lia and Aldous. What if it was worse than that? What if, somehow, it was Orson's fault they were caught?

He's your best friend, Draco thought.

I know. I don't want to believe it either. But what about magic? Could Kain have made him talk? Jacob thought, scanning the tunnel for Lia's hiding spot as he walked.

But if that was what had happened, why hadn't Orson told him the truth? And how had he escaped?

Jacob had nearly reached the end of the tunnel. The ground led upward. He saw a glimmer of light from the opening. Had Lia come this far?

Something brushed his face. He batted it away, then realized what it was — the stone, still in the pouch he had worn around his neck. It looked as if Lia had simply taken it off and hung it on a bit of rock. As if she meant to come back for it.

Strange.

He worked the pouch open, pulling the stone out. The moment it touched his skin, it started to glow, then grew warm.

He rested it on his upturned palm. It swung like a compass needle, pointing directly to the tunnel opening. He followed it.

This time there were no guards around. He crept out, around the large boulder that blocked the entrance, into the clearing. Except for the boulder, he was in a wide, open area. It was evening now; there were bright stars dotting the shadowy sky.

The light stone grew almost unbearably hot in his hand, glowing brightly in the dark. It turned as he walked, pointing back the way he had come.

"That doesn't make any sense," Jacob muttered. He crouched, holding the lit stone in the tunnel opening, looking for some sign of the dark stone. "I just don't understand," he said aloud. "You have to help me."

The stone cooled slightly. He reached farther into the tunnel. It cooled more. As he pulled it back toward himself, it grew warmer, then hotter still as he held it out to the clearing. He walked into the clearing again, around the large boulder. The stone cooled.

The boulder? He turned back to it, holding the stone close to its surface. The stone grew hotter.

Closer. The stone burned his hand.

He dropped it. It flew to the boulder and stuck there, held by some invisible force.

The earth shook. Jacob backed away. The boulder split open like a log struck by an ax.

Jacob pressed himself against the cliff face, but now it was quiet. The boulder lay open before him. When the dust settled, he saw his light stone on the ground between the two halves. Beside it, a hand span away, was a matching stone. The same curved dragon's tooth shape, but black instead of white. If the two were placed together, they'd form a perfect circle.

Hands trembling, he reached for them. Was this it? His chance to bring the two halves of the comet stone together, at last?

He lifted the stones. The dark stone was heavier than the light one. The moment he touched it, he felt the power in it. The voice he'd heard before, when he was holding the light stone, had only been an echo of this. He'd used the light stone once, so its power was gone, for him. But the dark stone … it had lain here, waiting. Waiting for him.

And he realized it didn't want to be joined to the light stone. To join it would be to change it. It had power in itself, just the way it was. It was perfect, all by itself.

With this, he could defeat Kain and Lord Manning. He'd be a hero — the man his father had always wanted him to be. He could even bring his father back from the land of the dead, to witness his victory. He saw it all, as clearly as if it were real.

Jacob! Draco thought.

He blinked. How long had he stood there, holding the two comet stones, lost in visions of his own glory? His torch had burned down and the sky was dark.

Jacob thought of Aldous' warnings. The dark stone would grant any wish, but twist it. Jacob felt the power in the stone, but it was not the sort of power he wanted.

Jacob had to join the stones now, no matter how strong the urge to take the dark stone and use it. He had to join them now, or he'd never have the willpower to do it. Using all his strength, he slowly brought the stones together.

There was a flash of light …

CHAPTER SIX | Betrayal

And then nothing.

Jacob stared at the comet stone. He pulled the two halves apart, then pushed them together. Nothing. He might as well have clinked two pebbles together. *I don't understand,* he sent to Draco.

Maybe it only works when the comet is in the sky, Draco thought.

Of course. That made sense. That was why the pull of the light stone had gotten stronger over the past few weeks. It was seeking out the dark stone before the comet's return. He only had to keep the stones safe until the comet returned, two weeks from now.

He placed the light stone back in its pouch and hung it around his neck. Its weight was comforting and both familiar. The dark stone, he placed in his pocket.

It took a long time to walk the length of the tunnel back to the cave. When he got there, he felt exhausted.

Orson paced back and forth in front of a lit fire. "Where have you been? It's been hours!" He stopped suddenly, staring at Jacob, eyes wild. "Did you find it?"

"I did," Jacob said, taking a step back. He pulled the pouch from around his neck.

He should tell Orson about the dark stone. Somehow, his mouth didn't want to form the words. His free hand crept into his pocket.

Orson snatched the pouch from Jacob and opened it, checking that the light stone was inside. "Good, this is good," he said. "We're running out of time. But Lord Manning's men are moving off the mountain. Maybe now we can hunt for the dark stone in peace." His words came out fast, falling over each other.

"I was right. She hid it in the tunnel," Jacob said, making his words slow and clear. "Why did she do that, do you think? Unless someone came in after her. Funny, isn't it? It's as if Lord Manning knew where she'd be hiding."

"Did you hear what I said?" Orson asked. "We can find the dark stone." He held the pouch out to Jacob. "Make it lead you."

Jacob kept his hands by his side. "First tell me how they found her," he said. "Tell me how Lord Manning's men knew about the tunnel."

"You're wasting time," Orson said. "I told you, getting the dark stone is the best way to help Lia and Aldous."

"I *already* found the dark stone!" Jacob said, pulling it from his pocket and thrusting it in Orson's face. "What I want is the truth."

The stone flared briefly, rays of light escaping from between Jacob's fingers.

Orson's eyes widened. "You found it," he whispered. He bared his teeth in a grin. "The truth? Kain wants this stone, and I'm going to bring it to him." He drew his sword.

Jacob stared. He knew he should do something, but he felt too betrayed to act. "This isn't you," he said.

Orson raised his sword. "You can give me the stone," he said. "Or I can take your hand with it."

It was a nightmare. It had to be.

"Do it then," Jacob said, still staring at his friend. "Cut off my hand."

Orson's face twisted. His sword shook in his hand. Then his face went blank and he swung the blade. Jacob pulled his hand back just in time.

He staggered back, looking for something to defend himself with, and fell against the woodpile. He grabbed a study branch, holding it in his uninjured arm.

"Think it through, Jacob," Orson said. "I've got a sword. A stick won't help you."

"You were the one who taught me to fight," Jacob said, holding the branch out in front of him. "A knight never gives up. You said that."

They circled each other, weapons outstretched.

"You're not a knight," Orson said. He struck with his sword.

When Jacob moved to block, Orson whirled away, then hit Jacob across the back with the flat of his sword.

Already off-balance, Jacob crashed to the cave floor. He tasted blood. The dark stone skidded out of his hand, towards the fire pit.

Help — I need help. He sent the thought not to Draco, who was too big to enter the cave, but to any birds that might be nearby.

Orson grabbed the stone. He held it up for Jacob to see. "You won't be able to follow me," he said. "But just in case, I'll make sure."

Jacob watched helplessly as Orson raised his sword again. Something crashed across his head, then the world went dark.

CHAPTER SEVEN
Lord Manning's Puppet

Jacob woke in the dark. He didn't know where he was or what had happened, but his body told him to fight. He struck out with his arms and legs, thrashing wildly.

You're awake! Draco's voice came crashing into his brain.

Jacob lifted his head, then dropped it again as pain seared across his skull. Something felt rough against his cheek — the cave floor. He tried to remember. Was it his turn to watch? Had Orson let him oversleep again?

Orson!

Jacob was sprawled on the cave floor. The fire had burned low. Orson was gone and the stones as well.

Slowly, Jacob sat up. *How long … ?*

Hours, Draco thought. *It's nearly morning.*

Did you stop Orson? Jacob thought. *I asked the birds for help…* Jacob paused as the reality of his friend's betrayal sank in.

They slowed him down for a bit, then he did something with the stones. After that, they weren't able to get near him, and neither was I. Lucky for him. Jacob had never heard such cold rage in Draco's mind.

You can't kill him, Jacob thought, responding to the rage, not the dragon's words. *Somewhere in there, it's still Orson.*

Or was it? What if Kain had used magic to make someone look like Orson? The real Orson could be held prisoner, or worse.

Or else Orson was under a spell, with Kain in control of his mind. It made sense — more sense than Orson's betrayal. But even if Jacob was right, he was no wizard. He didn't know how to bring his friend back.

Jacob closed his eyes. There was still so much to do. All he wanted was for the world to go away, just for a moment, before he had to move again.

It had been better, really, when he didn't remember where he was.

Jacob pushed himself to his feet. His stomach lurched but held.

I'm fine, he thought, in response to Draco's wordless concern.

You're not, Draco thought. *But come outside. I'm here now.*

Jacob crawled out of the cave.

Draco hovered in the sky nearby, early dawn behind him. The snow still held Orson's footprints. They were wide-spaced, like he'd been running.

Running. Not Jacob's strength at the best of times; impossible now. He could barely walk. He had other gifts, though.

He followed Orson's tracks along the snowy ledge, to where the ledge widened. There were more footprints there. *He had help*, Jacob thought. *A man met him here, with two horses.* The tracks showed that Orson and the other man had mounted the horses, then left together. Jacob followed the tracks a short distance. They had headed down the mountain, riding hard.

Find him, if you can, Jacob thought, sending the request to any birds close enough to hear. They might not be able to get near Orson, but at least they could tell Jacob how far Orson had gone.

Orson had said he was bringing the stones to Kain, but where was Kain?

We'll hide in the forest, until we figure out what to do next, Jacob thought. *I want to get off this mountain.*

Draco landed on the wide ledge so Jacob could mount. And then they were off, the motion of Draco's wings numbing Jacob's mind.

He dozed.

In his dream, Jacob was Draco. His wings beat the air, his muscles clenched and unclenched. He heard voices. *We're coming, young one. You will not be the last.* He flew and flew until the Earth was a tiny speck far below him, but he could not find the source of the voices. The thin air made him dizzy. He fell.

Jacob woke, sweating. He clutched at Draco's saddle, pushing himself upright.

Cold wind on his face helped banish the dream. He wished he could ask Aldous what it meant. He felt lost without Orson, Lia and Aldous. Lord Manning and Kain had taken them all, and Jacob didn't know how to get them back.

Chosen One! We found him! The bird sent Jacob a picture of Orson's camp, seen from high above. Jacob knew that place. Orson was camped in the Great Forest, in a site they'd used before.

How close can you get me? Jacob asked Draco.

The dragon was silent for a moment. *Twenty dragon-lengths*, he thought, finally. *That was as close as I could get to him because of the dark stone.*

Draco couldn't get near Orson, all because of Orson's wish on the dark stone. But the stone's power might not keep Jacob away. Orson wouldn't be expecting Jacob, so surprise would be on his side.

When Draco landed, there was little to say. *I'll be careful*, Jacob promised. He set off toward Orson's camp. Orson might be stronger, but Jacob was the better woodsman — even with his bad leg, he moved through the forest without making a sound.

Jacob sent birds to find Lia and Aldous. There was no chance of him rescuing them by himself, but he wanted to know what was happening.

Slowly, Jacob approached the camp. "You should have killed him," he heard when he got close. It wasn't Orson's voice.

Jacob crept to the edge of the campsite and watched. Orson crouched near a campfire, poking at it with a stick like he always did. A rabbit was roasting on a spit. It smelled wonderful.

"I didn't need to," Orson said quietly. "Besides, he was unarmed. A knight shows mercy."

Bad as things were, Jacob couldn't help grinning at that. He'd been right. The real Orson was still in there, somewhere.

The other man, wearing a guard's uniform, paced. Both horses were tied to a tree.

"You know what your problem is?" the guard asked. "You do whatever Kain wants, but you can't think for yourself." He smirked. "I guess that's the point, though, isn't it?"

Orson grunted.

"Filth and maggots! Stuck here for days with the wizard's brainless puppet. Kain should have told you to give the stones to me. We'd be halfway to the castle by now."

"He didn't," Orson said shortly. "Kain told me to deliver the stones to him at the castle, five nights from now. So I will."

"Well he didn't think you'd get your hands on the stones so fast, did he? You know he'd gladly take them sooner. Why wait?"

Jacob's head swam. He thought of the dark stone, of how powerful it was, of how he had held it for a short time. It could be his again. All he had to do was take it from Orson.

"Five nights from now," Orson repeated.

Jacob shook his head to clear it. He wasn't going to let the dark stone force him to act.

"Filth and maggots! Just give me the stones," the guard said. He drew his sword.

Orson sprang to his feet, sword ready before the other man could move. "No," he said.

"Then I'll take them." The guard swung at Orson, but he was too slow. Orson's blade blocked his easily, then slid forward and through his guts.

Jacob gasped, but the guard's cry hid it. Orson pulled his sword out. The man dropped to the ground. So much for mercy.

Orson wiped his blade clean, then stepped over the guard's body. "Five nights from now," he repeated.

Jacob shadowed Orson for days. Orson traveled faster, on horseback, but he always camped early in the day. It seemed that he was determined to make the two-day journey back to Lord Manning's castle last a full five days. That gave Jacob plenty of time each day to catch up with Draco.

All he needed was for Orson to let his guard down for a short time. Just long enough for Jacob to sneak in, grab the stones, and be gone. Then, with the stones to help him, he could rescue Lia and Aldous.

The birds had told him Lia and Aldous were in Lord

Manning's castle. With their help, he could figure out a way to get Orson back.

All the needed was a chance. But it never came.

Jacob watched Orson at night, waiting for him to sleep. The first night, he stood and paced silently in the woods while Orson crouched by his campfire, then sat, but never lay down. Jacob woke up the next morning, slumped against a tree, to the sound of Orson breaking camp.

The next night, with Draco's help, Jacob stayed awake. It didn't help. Orson never slept. Maybe it was the result of Kain's spell, but it seemed that Orson wasn't going to let his guard down at all.

Jacob needed a new plan.

CHAPTER EIGHT | Journey to the Castle

The sun had just risen, casting long shadows and painting the sky red. In the distance, Jacob saw the small market town that lay outside Lord Manning's castle walls. Behind the walls, a hill rose up, long steps leading to the castle's main doors.

Jacob had spent the night in a barn near the town — more comfortable lodgings than he was used to. Before dawn, he had made his way to the main road. Now he planned to ambush Orson on the way into town.

He had thought of leaping out of a tree to knock Orson from his horse, but there were no trees over the road. He'd have to hide deeper in the woods. He stared into the trees, looking for a likely place.

A man loomed up in front of him. Jacob dodged, but strong hands grabbed him. He twisted, trying to get away.

"Jacob?"

He knew that voice, and the smell of whiskey that came with it. Jacob looked up into the concerned face of Orson's father.

"What are you doing here? Where's Orson?" Orson's father set Jacob down on his feet. It was no question where Orson got his large size. The blacksmith was nearly as tall as his son and he was broader through the shoulders.

"He's coming," Jacob said. He opened his mouth to continue, but the words dried up.

Orson's father grinned. "I was on my way to market, but that can wait," he said. "We'll have a pint together."

Jacob shook his head. "No, you don't understand," he said.

The old man's grin faded. "What's wrong, son? Did you boys have a fight? It's not about that elf girl, is it?"

"He's not himself," Jacob said. Then, when Orson's father only looked blankly at him, he tried again. "Orson's under Kain's control."

"No son of mine ... " Orson's father began. Galloping hoof beats interrupted him.

Jacob turned to see Orson, bearing down on them. His face was blank.

Jacob stared in horror as Orson galloped closer. "Stop!" Jacob shouted.

Orson didn't even blink, just kept coming. Jacob leaped out of the way, but Orson's father stood there, gaping at his son. His lips shaped Orson's name.

Jacob tackled the large man, knocking him to the side of the dirt road. The horse thundered by, inches away.

Orson's father sat up slowly.

"Are you all right?" Jacob asked.

"He'd have trampled us," Orson's father said, staring into space. "Me, his own Pa. And you, his best friend." His voice trembled.

"He's not himself," Jacob said. He moved in front of the man's blank gaze. "I told you. I think Kain's put a spell on him. Orson took ... something from me. It was something important, and now he's bringing it to Kain. We both know he'd never do that."

Orson's father took a long drink from his ever-present hip flask. For once, Jacob wasn't tempted to try to stop him.

The old man shuddered as he put the flask away. Colour flooded back into his face.

"What do we do, then? How do we get my son back?" Orson's father asked.

Jacob helped him to his feet. It felt strange, having an adult look to him for answers, especially when he didn't have any to give. He needed Aldous. Even Orson would have a better idea of how to break into Lord Manning's castle than Jacob did.

"I have to get into the castle," he said, finally. "That's where he's gone, that's where the comet stones are."

There was a glint in the blacksmith's eye that Jacob had seen before, usually when he'd had too much to drink. "Well then, my boy, we'd best get you inside," he said.

~

Jacob didn't see the guard right away, nor could he see what Orson's father stole. Suddenly the old man was running. The guard was right behind him.

Orson's father headed toward the alley where Jacob stood on a barrel. Jacob tightened his grip on the heavy club in his hands, ready.

Orson's father ran past Jacob. "Don't miss, boy!" he shouted.

"I don't plan to." Jacob said, swinging hard. The guard dropped to the ground. "Sorry," Jacob muttered.

"What're you saying sorry for?" Orson's father asked. He wasted no time. He had already undone the guard's sword-belt. He handed it to Jacob.

"Wasn't exactly a fair fight," Jacob said.

Orson's father snorted. "You've been listening to my son, with all his talk about knights. A fight doesn't have to be fancy. The best ones usually aren't. What matters is that you win. Now do you want this uniform or not?"

Jacob knelt down and helped pull the guard's uniform off. The man was taller than Jacob, but not too much so. The pants tucked into his boots, anyhow.

Too bad the guard wore no helmet. It would have made it harder to knock him out, but a helmet might have helped to hide Jacob's face.

Jacob hoped that not all the guards knew each other by sight. The uniform helped, but getting into the castle was still going to be a challenge. His limp gave him away.

Orson's father must have been thinking the same thing. "What we need now is a good brawl." He grinned. "I'll make sure you're not the only guard limping."

Orson's father charged out of the alley like a bee-stung horse. He knocked over two carts before anyone caught up with him.

It was hard to follow what happened, after that. Jacob saw food flying and vendors pulling hair. There was a lot of shouting and cursing.

Once the fight grew large enough, the guards showed up. Then Jacob joined in. He made a show of pulling apart a few fist fights and waving his sword. All the while, he kept working his way closer to the castle gates.

His chance came when the brawl died down. Some of the guards headed back up the hill to the castle. Jacob followed them.

True to Orson's father's promise, Jacob wasn't the only person with a limp.

CHAPTER NINE

The Dungeon and the Tower

Jacob's limp and the blood on his uniform attracted few stares on the way to the castle. No one stopped him. It seemed that wounded guards were nothing new here.

He followed the guards into the castle, then left them. The dungeon was below ground, so he searched for stairs. As Jacob headed down and down again, the halls started to look familiar. He and Orson had been imprisoned in Lord Manning's dungeon once before. That was where they had first met Aldous, who had also been a prisoner.

Aldous had been given the prophecy when he was young. Jacob thought about that, and what it might mean. Of everyone on Earth, Aldous had been chosen to hear a message from the stars. Maybe it was just an accident of birth, like Jacob being the Chosen One.

A guard stood in front of the entrance to the dungeon. "I have a message for the old man and the elf," Jacob said.

The guard shrugged. "Old man's in the usual cell," he said. "Kain's got the elf. You should know that." He peered at Jacob.

Jacob hesitated. "I'm new," he said.

The guard muttered something, but he still let Jacob through.

It wasn't hard to find Aldous. He was, indeed, in his old cell — the one Orson and Jacob had shared with him. He jumped up when he saw Jacob.

"What are you doing here?" Aldous asked.

"Rescuing you," Jacob said.

Aldous shook his head. "There's no time for that," he said. "Listen to me. You can't trust Orson. He's under Kain's control."

"I know," Jacob said. "He stole the comet stones."

"You found them both?" For the first time, Aldous's eyes lit up. "Then there's hope, after all."

Jacob shook his head. "You're not listening. Orson stole them. He brought them here, to Kain. We've lost, Aldous. All I want now is to rescue you and Lia, and get Orson back."

Aldous sighed. "I'm not sure there's anything you can do for Orson. This is deep magic. It's not an easy spell to cast. Nor, I suspect, to break."

"There has to be a way," Jacob said. "I'll get you out of here, first. We'll find the others together." He glanced around, locating the keys hanging on a hook on the wall. "Which one is it?" he asked. The keys all looked the same. He proceeded to try them in the lock, one at a time.

"You need to find the comet stones, Jacob. Nothing else matters. They must be joined when the comet returns. If you don't do that, Kain and Lord Manning win. Kain knows you'll waste time trying to save us." Aldous' voice was sharp. "You're doing what he wants you to do."

"I'm doing the right thing," Jacob said. He tried to ignore the tiny doubts in his mind. Maybe Aldous was right, maybe this was what Kain wanted.

With the third key, the lock sprang free. He opened Aldous' door. "Here's what I know," he said. "Together, we've faced down Lord Manning and Kain before. Alone, I don't stand a chance. Besides," and his voice wavered here. "Friends help each other."

Aldous nodded. "The prophecy chose you. It had its reasons. It may be that your good heart will lead you well in the end. But if Kain has Lia, hurry. He'll be trying to change her, as he did Orson."

Jacob's guts turned to ice. Lia, under Kain's control. Lia, marrying Lord Manning … a willing bride this time.

Turning his back on Aldous, he rushed past the other guard.

"Hey! Where are you going? What's the prisoner

doing out?" the other guard shouted. Too late, Jacob realized he should have walked, acted natural, given the guard no reason to look around. Behind him, there was a cry.

He turned just in time to see Aldous stab the guard in the neck with his own crossbow arrow. The guard fell, blood soaking his shirt.

"Don't just stand there. Run!" Aldous shouted, taking the dead guard's weapons. "They may have heard him."

Jacob heard footsteps echoing down the hallway, coming closer.

"I can take care of myself, boy. Go!" Aldous said.

Jacob ran, praying that he wasn't too late.

He found stairs and headed up, but he had no idea where to find Kain's tower. *Help me*, he sent, calling any birds in the area. *I need to find the wizard's tower.*

Where the stairs turned, a narrow window let in a strip of light. A sparrow winged by. *Go east*, the bird thought. *East and higher.*

So Jacob did, finding his way through the castle's turnings by following the birds' directions. They circled the castle, watching his progress through windows.

Guards coming your way, a crow warned him at one point, giving Jacob time to duck behind a curtain.

Finally, he came to the bottom of a circular stairway. No windows lined its walls. *Here*, a robin sent to Jacob. *Kain's room is at the top of the tower. He's not inside, only the elf.*

Jacob's heart rushed. He raced up the stairs, not bothering to be quiet about it. He ran up the curving steps until his lungs were tight and his brain half dizzy from the turns. The tower was hollow, the stairs wrapping around an empty space in the middle that turned into a frightening drop as Jacob went higher.

"Take your time," a familiar voice called from above. "I'll wait."

Knowing, but not wanting to believe, Jacob climbed the final steps slowly. He held his sword in front of him. The stairs led, at last, to a small platform. On the platform stood Orson, leaning against a heavy, wooden door.

Orson grinned to see Jacob, a grin that didn't reach his eyes. He shook his hair out of his face. The gesture was familiar but somehow wrong.

"She's inside," Orson said. He moved into a fighting stance. "But you'll have to get past me, first."

CHAPTER TEN | "Fight or Run"

Jacob stared at Orson. Lia was locked in Kain's tower room, behind that wooden door, and all he had to do to get to her was … to kill his best friend?

Seeing his confusion, Orson grinned even more widely. "Come on," he said. "You know you've always wanted to best me."

Jacob slowly lifted his sword, not pointing it at Orson, just holding it as a barrier between them. "Don't do this."

Orson's grin vanished. He leveled his sword at Jacob.

"Fight or run," he said.

And that did it. Something snapped inside Jacob. He was sick of running, sick of hiding and searching and waiting while Lord Manning and Kain picked off the people he loved one by one. Running wasn't an option anymore.

Jacob flew at Orson, his sword slicing the air.

Orson turned Jacob's attack aside with a flick of his wrist. "Too obvious, Jacob," he said. "I've told you. Don't show your moves before you make them."

Jacob swung again, only to find his sword locked against Orson's. "Your Pa's worried about you."

Something flickered in Orson's eyes, then died. He pulled away and twisted his body into an attack that Jacob barely managed to block.

"No one gets into this room. Kain's orders," Orson said.

"You don't take orders from Kain!" Jacob shouted. "You don't take orders from anybody. You're one of the most stubborn people I've ever met. So be stubborn now! Fight this." He forced his way onto the landing. Now he was level with Orson.

Orson attacked again, backing Jacob against the wall. But was it Jacob's imagination, or was Orson slowing down? Twice, he had hesitated before striking.

Otherwise, no point in lying to himself, Jacob would probably be dead by now.

"You're in there. I know you are," Jacob panted, as he backed away.

Orson ran at him.

Jacob raised his sword to meet Orson's, but instead he ducked down and stuck out his leg. Orson's blade grazed his arm, but the pain was worth it. Orson tripped, rolling down the stairs.

Jacob tried the door. Locked.

He closed his eyes, concentrating. Kain had used a different room, once, with a large window ... which Jacob had sent a dragon crashing through. *Are there windows?* he thought, asking the birds who had guided him to the tower.

None we can get through, a crow thought. He sent a picture of a small, narrow window with metal grating over it.

Orson was rushing back up the stairs now.

Is there any way in? Jacob thought, desperate now as he turned to face Orson.

The crow sent a picture of smoke drifting out through a vent in the roof.

I need you to get in and open the lock, Jacob thought. *Show me what it looks like and I'll tell you how.*

But Orson was on top of him now, stronger than before. He knocked Jacob's sword away and pressed the point of his own sword to Jacob's neck, pinning him against the wall. Jacob froze, staring into Orson's eyes.

The point of the sword was sharp against Jacob's throat. He tried not to breathe or swallow. He stared at Orson, willing him to remember who he was, who both of them were.

Orson's hand shook.

He hadn't killed Jacob. Why hadn't he killed him yet?

Suddenly, Orson's eyes went flat.

The crow, still listening to Jacob, shrieked a warning in Jacob's head. Instantly, Jacob projected the crow's voice into Orson's mind, the way he had once done with Lia. He felt the connection snap into place, just the way it had happened before.

But Lia was an elf. Orson wasn't. After only half a second, the connection was gone.

Then Orson's sword dropped from his hand. His eyes rolled up into his head, then he crumpled.

Jacob swallowed. He touched his throat, where the sword had been.

He knelt, slowly, to look at Orson. Blood ran from his friend's nose. Orson was breathing, but he didn't stir when

Jacob shook his shoulder. When Jacob peeled Orson's eyelids back, he saw only white. He flinched away.

What had he done?

Jacob didn't even notice that he was shaking until he stood up.

A crash came from behind Kain's locked door. Jacob reached for Orson's sword. The lock rattled. He got between Orson and the door, ready to face whatever came out.

The door burst open. A flood of birds flew into the stairwell, all chattering at once, blocking Jacob's view. He raised his sword with both hands, trying to shield his eyes with his forearm. *Clear out!* he thought, as hard as he could.

The birds scattered. Where they had been, standing in a swirl of drifting feathers, stood Lia. Her eyes flicked between Jacob and Orson. Then she flew into Jacob's arms, knocking him back against the railing.

"I knew it was you. I knew you'd come!" she said.

Jacob just held her tight, breathing in the wild-mint smell of her hair. She was safe, warm and solid in his arms. Whatever else had happened, she was safe.

Finally, she pulled away. "You're hurt," she said.

"I'm fine," Jacob said. "But Orson ... I used the mind speech to stop him. I ..."

Her eyes darkened. "Jacob, he tricked us," she said. "He pretended Lord Manning's men had him, and then he called to us to help him, in the cave. That's how we got caught."

"He's under a spell," Jacob said. "I don't know how Kain did it."

"I do," she said. "Because he tried it on me, too. But it doesn't work on elves."

"Then you can help him, right?" Jacob knelt beside Orson. "You can bring him back."

She knelt, too, but slowly. She brushed a hand over Orson's forehead, concentrating, then bit her lip. "What Kain did … it was magic. There's no way for me to heal a magic spell. I can help with his other injuries, but what if he wakes up and attacks us again?"

"We can't just leave him," Jacob said.

"I don't think we have a choice," Lia asked. "I care about Orson, too. But I don't think Orson's coming back. Jacob, you want to help him. But ask yourself — is he an enemy or a friend?"

"A friend," Jacob said firmly.

Lia shrugged, but let it go. "We have to get those comet stones. I know what's going on, now. Kain was gloating. The stones can't be destroyed, but they can be joined together, and that's the only way to kill him."

She placed a hand on Jacob's forehead, meeting his eyes.

Jacob didn't object to her unspoken offer of help. In seconds, he felt her healing warmth flow into him.

The weakness in his knees had nothing to do with his injuries.

"I tried putting the stones together," Jacob said, after she let go. "Nothing happened."

"Dragon fire," she said. "That's why he's killing the dragons. Part of the reason. Dragon fire is the only way to join them together, and it can only be done when the comet is in the sky."

"So if we fail, Kain lives forever," Jacob said.

"Or until the comet comes back." Lia nodded. "There's not much time. I left the light stone in the cave tunnel. Get Draco to fly you back there and get it, then find the other one. Be fast."

A chilling laugh echoed up the stairwell. Kain strode into view, moving soundlessly. "But my dear, there's no need," he said. "I have both comet stones right here." He held the dark stone up in one hand and muttered something in a strange language. Jacob's body locked into place. He couldn't move, not even a fingertip.

Then his body, still frozen, floated up. Kain flicked a wrist and Jacob zoomed out over the railing, to hang suspended in midair. His stomach lurched, seeing the long drop to the floor.

"I don't want to kill him," Kain said to Lia. His tone was calm. It didn't match his torn robes and matted hair. "But I will if I have to. If I drop him now, he'll shatter like glass. Of course, that might be kinder. It's your choice. If you do as I say, he lives a while longer, at least until I find out more about how his bird speech works. Fight me and he dies now."

Slowly, her gaze on Kain, Lia nodded.

"Well done," Kain said. He gripped Lia's jaw. "Lord Manning still wants you, for some reason, and it suits me to keep him happy for now. You'll be married on Claw Mountain when the comet returns. I'd have liked to give him a willing bride, but your brain is stronger than your friend's." He kicked Orson. Orson groaned. "No matter. An unwilling bride will do."

Jacob was sure he saw Orson's eyes open, just for a split second, to glare at Kain.

CHAPTER ELEVEN | Dragon's Return

Bones lined the bottom of the pit. The bones had crunched when Kain lowered Jacob in, and they poked into him now.

Jacob still had no control over his body. He felt like he had no control over his mind, either. He tried again and again to call for Draco but Draco didn't answer. All Jacob could do was lie still and wait. Outside his cell, day changed to night and stars appeared, far away through the metal grating.

Lord Manning and his men would be leaving soon,

heading up Claw Mountain, and there was nothing he could do about it. He counted up the days in his mind. In one short week, the comet would return.

Hours passed. Finally, Jacob was able to drag himself into a sitting position. By morning, he could stand and walk, but he still couldn't reach Draco with his mind.

The days passed slowly. He thought often of Orson and Aldous and Lia, wondering where they were and what they were doing. Each morning, a woman from the castle threw bread down. Each morning, she lowered water to him in a pail. He'd been warned not to try to grab the rope when it came down. "I'll cut it," she had said. "And then you'll not get water. A body can't live many days like that."

Day after day, Jacob tried to contact Draco. But Kain must have done something with the dark stone to keep Jacob from calling for help. Kain had to be keeping the birds away, too. The pit was in a wooded area, but no birds came.

Night after night, Jacob kept watching the stars. His narrow view of the sky didn't take in the star sign Draco, but he watched anyhow, for some hint of the comet.

On the seventh morning, Jacob woke before dawn. He watched the sky slowly lighten. After his bread and water came down, he reached for Draco with his mind, more from habit than hope.

At last, he found him.

Jacob! You're alive! The dragon's joy spread through Jacob's body. He couldn't help grinning.

I'm alive, and I need your help, he thought. Jacob had come up with a plan days ago. *Here's what I want you to do.*

~

By the time Draco returned, it was early afternoon. Jacob paced back and forth.

I brought him, Draco thought. He sounded pleased with himself.

Orson's father appeared, leaning on the grating. "Dear God in Heaven," he muttered. "Never again. If I never do that again, it'll be too soon."

"Down here!" Jacob called.

Orson's father startled. "Filth and maggots! There's someone down there. Is that you, Jacob? You won't believe the morning I've had." His words were slurred. "Attacked by birds. They came right into the house, knocked over my whiskey, and herded me out. Then ... out front ..." His voice faded.

"It's all right," Jacob said. "They're only trying to help

me. I asked them to bring you to me. Do you have your tools?"

"The maggot-ridden birds pecked at me until I went into my shop and got them," Orson's father said. "Then they made me get on the dragon." He shuddered.

The birds are bringing rope. They'll be here soon, Draco thought.

"I'm sorry," Jacob lied. He was sorry Orson's father had been scared, but there were lives at risk. "Listen, I need you to open the grating. Can you do that?"

He had thought it through. The dragon's fire might melt the bars, but not without the risk of burning Jacob. It wasn't likely that Draco would be able to get a grip on the metal grating or pull it free without caving the whole thing in. Jacob needed a human's help. Orson's father was his best bet.

"Eh? Sure, I can do that, right enough." Orson's father left, then returned with a sledgehammer. Working at the fastenings with sledgehammer and metal rods, he soon had it free.

By then, the birds had arrived. Orson's father lowered the long rope down to Jacob, who tied it around his waist.

With the blacksmith's help, Jacob was out of the pit in minutes. Orson's father pulled him into a crushing hug.

"Did you find Orson?" the old man finally asked,

stepping back. Hope made his voice raw.

"Er, yes," Jacob said, untying the rope from around his waist. "But Kain still has him." What else to say? They fought? Orson tried to kill him? He very nearly killed Orson?

Orson's father looked at him for a long moment. "I see." He sighed, then started coiling up the dropped rope. "We'll find a way to get him back. But if I read the sky right, you'd best get up Claw Mountain now."

He said nothing about Orson.

"I'll do everything I can," Jacob said, helplessly. Orson's father nodded.

Jacob climbed onto Draco's back.

"Here," Orson's father said. He held up the rope, neatly coiled. "Never know when this might come in handy. I've got a dagger here, too ... it's no sword, but it'll do in a pinch." He passed Jacob the long knife out of his belt.

Jacob carefully stuck it down his boot. "Thank you," he said.

Orson's father nodded. "Use it on the wizard."

As Draco took off, Jacob could hear Orson's father muttering to himself. Jacob could have sworn he heard the words "never drink again." But then he and Draco were gone, and the words were swallowed by the wind.

CHAPTER TWELVE | "Fly Wild"

Jacob watched the stars as they flew, seeking Draco, the star-dragon. When the comet entered the star-dragon, that was when he had to act. That was when the real Draco had to use his fire to join the two stones together.

Before that, Jacob had to rescue Lia from Lord Manning, find Kain, and steal the comet stones from him. And none of this began to deal with the problem of Orson.

Jacob wondered where Aldous was. He hadn't seen

him since the dungeon. He trusted Aldous to have won his fight with the guard, but had he gotten out of the castle?

Draco dropped a few feet lower. Jacob's stomach lurched. *"You need to get off,"* Draco thought. His mind-voice sounded strained.

What's wrong? Are you hurt? Jacob hadn't noticed any injuries, but maybe something had happened to Draco while they were apart.

No. Kain's calling me. He's using the dark stone, I can feel it. I don't think I'm going to be able to resist for long, Draco thought, drawing closer to the mountain.

Why does he want you there? You're a danger to him, Jacob thought. *It's your fire that he fears most.*

There was a long pause before Draco answered. *I don't think ... I'm a danger to him.* His mind-voice was small, fading away, even though Jacob was right there on his back. *He wants me to land.*

But you're not going to, right? Right? Jacob pressed hard with his mind. Something was wrong. He was losing his connection to Draco.

Draco didn't answer. It was gone. Their bodies were in contact, but their minds weren't.

Draco! Jacob sent. *Fight it!*

It was no good. Draco changed course toward the

clearing. Already, Jacob could see the tiny shapes that had to be Lord Manning and his men. His throat dried up. "Draco, no," he whispered.

Draco was going to land and they'd both be killed. Unless … if he could just buy a few minutes, maybe he could think of something. Some way to save them.

He scanned the cliff face. This was where he had found the cave. If they got closer … yes, there it was. The ledge. And Jacob still had the rope that Orson's father had used to pull him out of the pit; it was coiled on Draco's saddle.

"Can you get me close to the ledge?" he asked. Draco seemed to understand, because they turned slightly toward it. Jacob tied the rope to Draco's saddle. The other end, he'd just have to grip.

"Fly wild," he told Draco. "You're trying to fight him, and he knows it. You don't have to go straight there."

Draco let out a roar but did as Jacob asked. His flight path drew him ever closer to the mountaintop, but he veered in all directions.

Jacob's hands were sweaty. Not good for someone who was about to slide down a rope. He wiped them on his pants. "Just get me close," he said to Draco. "That's all you have to do." That, and not crush him against the cliff face.

Jacob tested his knot once more, then slid off Draco, holding onto the rope. He slid down faster than he'd hoped and barely managed to catch himself. Then he was hanging below Draco, much like a toy on the end of a rope. The ledge came up fast. Jacob forced himself to swing back and forth.

Draco roared again. Jacob couldn't tell if he was angry at Kain's control or Jacob's plan. Draco did as Jacob asked, though, and brought him close to the cliff face.

"Closer," Jacob whispered.

When he saw his chance, Jacob let go of the rope and flew free.

He hit the cliff face with a bone-shaking crunch. He bounced off, rolling when he hit the ground. A large rock barely stopped him from falling off the ledge. His vision went dark, then light again, as he struggled to hang on. His skull throbbed.

Above him, Draco roared once more, then flew higher, rope still trailing.

Jacob hurt pretty much everywhere, but nothing seemed to be broken. He didn't trust himself to stand yet. He rolled back onto the ledge, panting.

Stars wheeled overhead. Jacob strained his eyes, looking for some sign of the bright, fiery comet.

He slowly sat up, then got to his feet. The tunnel was his best bet for getting to the surface without being seen. It would be dark, but he'd been through it twice before. He thought he could feel his way through the tunnel.

He made his way into the cave. He hesitated, then went in, groping his way around the cave wall. The walls grew close when he entered the tunnel. He walked on, stumbling and crawling when he had to. Inch by inch, he felt his way through a darkness that threatened to swallow him.

His heartbeat echoed in his ears. It seemed like hours passed before he felt ice under his fingers — the frozen stream. A lifetime later, the tunnel sloped upward. Finally, a dim light reached him. The opening.

He rushed, eager for light and air. Jacob breathed deeply. He didn't even want to blink.

The meadow was there, just as he remembered, and the large boulder that had broken in two. Sitting on one of the boulder halves was Aldous. "Come on then," he said, as if it were perfectly normal for Jacob's head to pop out of a rock wall. "We haven't got much time."

Jacob crawled out. "Kain has Draco! He's controlling him, and we can't mind-speak anymore. And Lia's there, Lord Manning is going to marry her tonight, up on the mountain." The words fell out too fast, tripping his tongue.

"But you're here. And so am I," Aldous said. "And we've done well to make it this far. I think we have it in us to do more yet, don't you?"

A strange thing to say. Jacob looked at Aldous. His face was calm in the starlight but more lined than Jacob remembered.

"The comet is here," Aldous said. "Soon it will enter the star-dragon. We have much to do before then."

"You've seen it?" Jacob asked, looking up. He saw only stars.

"There." Aldous pointed just above the horizon. There was a milky glow, little more than a smudge. It certainly wasn't the giant fireball Jacob had expected.

"That's the comet?" Jacob asked. Such a little thing, to bring so much change.

"It is," Aldous said. "We have an hour, at best."

"Then let's go."

The meadow led to a passage. Aldous seemed to know the way. It wasn't long before they heard voices, and not long after that before Aldous waved Jacob to the ground. "Stay low," he said.

Jacob crept forward and peered over a small ridge. He saw a wide, flat, open area. Draco was on the far side, staring blank-eyed at Kain, who was chanting. Closer to Jacob, Lord Manning and Lia stood, surrounded by a ring of guards. Lia's hands were tied behind her back.

"You've served your purpose," Lord Manning told her. The scar Jacob had given him in their last encounter pulled his left eye tight. "Kain thought the dragon might attempt a rescue, even without its pet boy, and it did. The dragon must die, but you need not. For the last time, elf! Marry me."

Lia must have murmured something, because Lord Manning leaned in closer. "What was that?" he asked.

She spat in his ruined face.

"Kill her," he said coldly, stepping back. He wiped his face with his sleeve.

The guard behind Lia shifted, and in the moonlight, Jacob saw his profile. It was Orson.

CHAPTER THIRTEEN
Through a Dragon's Eyes

Jacob watched in horror as Orson shoved Lia forward and raised his sword.

"No!" Jacob shouted, but the sword was already falling.

Orson sliced the ropes that bound Lia's hands. Quickly, she spun away from him.

Lord Manning stared in Jacob's direction. "Kill him," he said to his guards. Five of them rushed toward Jacob, who scrambled to stand up.

"Jacob! Catch!" Orson shouted. He pulled something

from around his neck, swung it twice, and launched it at Jacob. Jacob caught it, fumbling. It was the pouch containing the light stone.

"I'll explain later!" Orson called.

Lord Manning drew his own sword and rushed at Orson, but Orson was ready for him. Their swords met, then erupted into a blur of movement.

Jacob drew the dagger from his boot. It wasn't going to be enough, not against five men. The only advantage he had was height — he was on the ridge, they were racing up it. He picked up a fist-sized rock and hurled it at the first guard. His aim was good; the guard went down, his face covered in blood.

He threw another rock. This one flew wide.

From behind him, Aldous threw another rock, taking down the guard that Jacob had just missed. "You need to reach Draco," he said. "Go!"

Jacob ran down the hill, letting his legs carry him faster than he could control. When he got close to the third guard, he dropped and rolled, knocking the guard flying. At the bottom of the hill, Jacob climbed back to his feet. He broke into a limping run.

"Jacob!" Lia shouted.

"Come with me," he called. He heard her fall into place behind him. They soon passed Orson and Lord

Manning, still deep in battle.

"Stay back! He's mine!" Lord Manning shouted at his guards.

Lia was faster than Jacob. She soon overtook him.

As they neared Draco, Kain's back was to them. The teeth he had collected from his victims shone in his black, matted hair. He held the dark stone up to the sky, taunting the stars. He chanted harsh-sounding words that made no sense to Jacob.

Draco lay before Kain, head on the ground, neck

outstretched. Jacob reached for Draco's mind again, but failed. The dragon's eyes drifted shut.

At the same time, Kain's chanting began to change. "Dragon's blood, to me. Dragon's strength, to me," he said, repeating it over and over, while he slipped the dark stone into a pouch around his neck.

From his belt Kain drew a long, curved sword. He moved closer to Draco, blade raised high.

Lia hurled herself into him. She was too light to knock him over, but he stopped chanting, just for a second. That was the chance Jacob needed.

Draco! he screamed with his mind. *Draco, wake up! You have to move!*

Jacob? The dragon's mind-voice sounded far away. Too faint.

Jacob fell to his knees beside the dragon's head. He pressed his forehead against Draco's warm scales. *Hear me*, he thought.

He pushed with his mind. He remembered how it felt when he was connected with Draco and they were flying. He thought about the way Draco's wings beat. He willed them to move, willed Draco's muscles to stir, and suddenly there was a feeling like falling.

When he recovered, he was inside the dragon — his mind in Draco's body. That massive body was his to control.

Jacob-in-Draco's-body lifted his head, his neck rising up in a movement that felt snake-like. The world looked different through wide-set dragon eyes. Slowly, he got to his four feet.

He heard a scream. Lia. She was staring in horror at the crumpled, bleeding body of a boy. Jacob's body. Kain stood over it, bloody sword outstretched, but dragon-Jacob didn't feel any pain. What he felt was strong. Strong and angry and very, very powerful. He flexed his claws, getting the feel of them.

He sensed Draco's mind, as well, deep inside, but Draco wasn't ready to fight yet. Jacob was.

Kain ran, stumbling backwards to get away from Jacob-the-dragon.

Jacob opened his mouth and sent a stream of fire over the wizard.

Kain spoke a word and the fire went around him, as though he held an invisible shield.

Jacob's eyes narrowed. He crouched, ready to spring. If fire didn't work, claws might.

Lia crouched over boy-Jacob's body. When she stood, Jacob saw that she held his dagger in one hand, the light stone in the other. She faced Kain, eyes blazing.

The wizard didn't see her. He was concentrating on the dragon. Lia launched herself at Kain for the second time. This time, she clamped herself around him, legs tight around his waist, one arm across his shoulder. She brought the dagger to Kain's neck.

"Do it," Kain said, sneering. "See what happens."

Jacob couldn't attack Kain with Lia so close. He growled, willing her to get out of the way. She hacked with the dagger, then leapt off Kain, running. The wizard felt his throat, and his eyes widened. "The dark stone!" he shouted.

Lia had both comet stones. Kain turned and sent a bolt of lightning after her, but Jacob pounced in front of it, catching it on a foreleg. It hurt, but not enough to slow him down.

He sent another burst of fire over the wizard. Again, the wizard deflected it. It didn't matter. Now, all Jacob wanted was to give Lia time.

Jacob-the-dragon jumped, pinning Kain under his claws. He flexed again. Aldous had said the only way to kill the wizard was by joining the comet stones together, but surely it was possible to hurt Kain. Jacob would very much like to do that.

Aldous battled his way across Lord Manning's few remaining guards, trying to reach Lia. Suddenly he froze. His eyes widened, staring at boy-Jacob's body on the ground.

Jacob wished there was some way to make them understand — he was fine, he was here. Jacob was inside Draco.

Jacob-the-dragon roared, startling Aldous into motion. Lia struggled to get the dark stone out of Kain's pouch. She finally did, then fit the two pieces together. She held them up, clasped in a fist. "Do it, Draco!" she shouted. "It's time!" She closed her eyes.

But Jacob couldn't. He'd seen what dragon fire did to a body. He couldn't burn her, not even if it meant saving all of their lives. He shook his giant head back and forth.

Pinned as he was, Kain managed to send a burst of lightning into the soft underside of Jacob's throat. That hurt. Jacob sank a claw through Kain's chest, which should have killed the wizard but somehow didn't. Kain, pale and gasping, still managed to laugh. "You can't do it, can you?" he said. "Then I win."

Aldous reached Lia. He took the two stones from her hand. "This is mine to do," he said gently. "Your skills are needed elsewhere."

He faced Jacob-the-dragon, holding the two stones joined together in his left hand. "Now," he said. "You know this is the only way."

And Jacob did. He looked deep into Aldous's eyes,

then breathed out the smallest stream of fire he could manage. He sent it over Aldous' arm.

Aldous screamed, then dropped to the ground, writhing. Out of his black and withered hand dropped the comet stone ... the two merged into one, dark and light twisting around each other.

And Kain disappeared. Jacob's claws rested on plain earth. It was as if the wizard had never been there.

Had he escaped again? Or was this what was supposed to happen? Jacob wished the prophecy had been clearer.

Lia rushed to boy-Jacob's side. Jacob saw the glow that meant she was using a lot of healing energy. It surrounded boy-Jacob's body, and he felt the tug of a faraway heartbeat. His own.

He felt a rush of thoughts from Draco's awakening mind — fear, shock, relief. Memories of flying, even of hatching. Dreams. Jacob's own face seen through wide-set eyes. Then things went dark.

CHAPTER FOURTEEN
"You Were a Good Man Once"

Jacob woke slowly. There was a terrible, burning pain across his chest. He felt small and weak. He opened his eyes.

"You're all right!" It was Lia's voice. Her face swam into focus, tear-streaked and pale as a stone in the moonlight.

The world seemed narrow. He only had human eyes, now.

"How very touching." Lord Manning's deep voice cut across the clearing. "Now tell me, what have you done with my wizard?"

Lia helped Jacob to sit up.

Draco still seemed stunned. Orson was a bleeding heap at Lord Manning's feet. Kain was nowhere to be seen. And Aldous — Aldous stood, slowly, his left arm hanging uselessly at his side. "Kain is here," he said to Lord Manning. "Inside me."

Lord Manning whirled about to face Aldous. "Explain yourself," he said. His remaining guards were clustered behind him.

"Kain is back where he belongs," Aldous said. "He is a part of me."

Lord Manning backed away, shaking his head. Jacob might have been shocked, too, except that he had just spent the past five minutes inside a dragon's body. After that nothing was terribly hard to believe.

"You were a good man once," Aldous said, softly. "So was I. It's not too late for you. Let us help our friend. Turn yourself in. The King is not without mercy."

"The King!" Manning's voice was bitter. "I should be King, not that weak fool. " He approached Aldous. "You say Kain is inside you. Then you have his power. We can join together, you and I." He held out his hand.

Aldous shook his head.

"So be it." Lord Manning struck Aldous, knocking him to the ground.

Why didn't he get up and fight back? Why didn't he throw bolts of energy, like Kain had?

"Bring the elf," Lord Manning said. His guards pulled Lia away from Jacob. She kicked, but there were three of them, and she was weak from healing Jacob.

"Leave her alone!" Jacob shouted.

"You stay down," Lord Manning said, pointing his sword at Jacob. Not that he could stand, anyhow. "I'll deal with you later. Perhaps we'll make your face match mine." He ran a finger along his scar.

Jacob reached with his mind for Draco, but the dragon's thoughts barely stirred. *"Help me!"* he thought, sending the call as wide as he could. There were few birds on the mountaintop.

A hawk swooped in, but one of Lord Manning's guards shot it with an arrow.

"Any more of that and the elf dies," Lord Manning said. He walked over to where Lia was being held. "You might have been my bride," he said. "But I find I've lost interest. Still, there's no reason why I shouldn't enjoy myself." He grabbed a fistful of her hair and crushed his mouth against hers. Jacob felt sick.

When Lord Manning pulled away, Lia spat at him again, but this time he only laughed. "Pin her down," he said to his guards.

No. This wasn't going to happen. *Draco!* Jacob screamed with his thoughts. He staggered to his feet.

I'm still here. The dragon's mind-voice was weak, but alert. Draco raised his head, taking in the scene.

Talk to me, Jacob thought. He took Draco's anger and fear, his panicked thoughts, and sent them into Lord Manning's mind, the way he had done twice before with bird speech.

Lord Manning's entire body went rigid. He fell to the ground, shaking. Blood streamed from his nose and mouth. Then, as Jacob watched in horror, he clutched at his chest and gasped.

He stilled, his face a pale gray, eyes staring blankly at the sky.

Dead.

The guards looked at each other.

"Get away from her." It was Orson's voice. He was blood-soaked and pale, but he stood, and the sword he pointed at the remaining guards didn't shake in his hand.

The guards ran.

The three of them, Jacob, Lia and Orson, looked at each other for a long moment. Then Orson dropped to one knee. Lia rushed to his side.

Jacob tried to step forward, but his legs wouldn't hold him. He sagged back, only to find Draco there, behind him, propping him up. He leaned against the dragon's warm scales. *Thank you,* he thought.

Jacob ... what you did ... Draco thought, and Jacob felt his confusion. Their link was strong, but it was no easy thing to have another mind controlling your body.

I don't know how it happened, Jacob thought. *I'm sorry. I'd never have done that to you by choice.*

You saved us. Draco's mind-voice was firm. *All of us.*

All of them. Lia still knelt beside Orson, but the glow

coming from her hands told Jacob that his friend would live. Aldous, though. Where was Aldous?

Jacob spotted the old man lying where Lord Manning had thrown him. He made his way to Aldous, afraid of what he might find.

Aldous was breathing fast and shallow, but at least he was still breathing. He raised his head when Jacob appeared. "You did it," he said.

Jacob lifted Aldous' shoulders so the old man could lean against him. "Lia will be here soon," he said. "Hold on."

Aldous shook his head. "There's nothing she can do. It's better that she not try," he said. "My years should have ended long ago." He fixed Jacob's eye with his own. "I know what you did. It was well done."

"Lord Manning?"

"Lord Manning earned his fate," Aldous said. "No, I speak of Draco and of the joining of the stones."

"I was … inside him," Jacob said. The wonder of it still hadn't caught up to him.

Aldous nodded. "Your powers have grown. But you mustn't …" A wet cough interrupted his words.

"I know," Jacob replied. "I won't do it again." Jacob hesitated. "You said Kain was inside you. What did you mean?"

"I am now as I was meant to be," Aldous said. He smiled, and his eyes wandered. "One soul, good and bad. I've made mistakes, Jacob, grave mistakes. But they are finished now."

"So Kain is gone?" Jacob had to know. The wizard had disappeared once, when Jacob was fighting him, only to come back more terrible than before.

"Kain was born out of me. From my greed. I was given a great gift when I found the comet stone, and I abused it, seeking to find a way to live forever. My actions split the stone and my soul at the same time. Now both are reunited." Aldous closed his eyes.

"So the prophecy … ?"

"Came when the stones split. I was never completely honest with you, Jacob, or with anyone. Too much shame." He sighed. "I'm tired, now."

"But you saved us," Jacob whispered, and he thought he saw the ghost of a smile pass over the old man's face.

"They're coming," Aldous said, clearly. He opened his eyes, then stared into the skies before his chest stopped moving.

Gently, Jacob laid Aldous down.

Orson approached, supporting Lia. He looked much healthier. Lia didn't. Her face was drawn and pale.

"She needs to rest, but she won't," Orson told them.

Then he saw Aldous' body and grew still.

Lia's face creased, then cleared. "Maggots," she said. "I wish you people would stop trying to die on me!" She dropped to her knees, laying her hands on Aldous' face.

Nothing happened.

Jacob took her hands and held them. "It's all right," he said. "Death is what he wanted."

She shook her head. "No." But she let Jacob pull her away.

It was Orson's idea to bury the dead guards and soldiers. Draco gouged a long pit out of the earth for Lord Manning and each of his fallen guards.

When the burial was done, Jacob stood a moment beside Lord Manning's grave. "Aldous said he was a good man, once," he said. "But I still don't want Aldous to lie here with them. It doesn't seem right." Reaching for Draco's mind with his own, he explained his idea.

CHAPTER FIFTEEN | The Way Home

A funeral pyre made a fitting end for Aldous. Dragon fire burned hot and fast; it didn't take long.

Jacob, Orson and Lia watched as the embers faded and the sky turned from black to deep blue. Lia was the first to notice. "Look," she said.

Draco was staring at the sky, his body arched.

Draco? Jacob thought, reaching. The dragon's mind was awash in other voices. Jacob had to pull back. "Something's happening," he said, leaning on Orson for support.

Against the pre-dawn sky, three dark shapes appeared. Jacob squinted, trying to make them out.

"Those aren't dragons, are they?" Orson asked.

"They're coming," Jacob whispered to him, repeating Aldous's last words.

Draco flew to intercept the new arrivals. Jacob tried not to listen in, but the dragon's joy was too great. Thoughts leaked through. *In hiding ... so sorry ... together again ...*

"How is this possible?" Lia asked. "I thought his mother said he was the last."

"The last male dragon," Jacob said. "If Kain had killed him, the species would have died out. These others . . ." He let himself listen in. "They were in hiding. Dragon magic. I don't understand, but somehow they went . . . away. Not in this world. Until Kain died. It was dangerous, whatever they did. Most of them . . . didn't make it."

Lia's eyes widened. "Dragon magic. But an egg would never survive a journey like that. Draco's mother wouldn't leave him; that's why she stayed."

Jacob felt a wave of sadness from Draco and realized that he had been listening to Jacob's thoughts as well. *She'd be proud of you,* Jacob thought. He knew it was true.

"You saved us," Lia said, leaning against Jacob.

"I didn't," he said. "Aldous did. He's the hero, not me."

She smiled. "I remember it differently."

He took her hand. Lia didn't pull away.

It had been a long, strange night, and Jacob knew it was going to take a long time to sort through what had happened. "Your father will want to see you," he said to Orson. "And I'm more than ready to leave this place."

Will you and your friends carry us? he thought, reaching for his link to Draco. He didn't try to mind-speak with the new dragons yet. He wasn't ready to share his thoughts with strangers, not tonight. There would be time for all that.

Happily, Draco answered.

They were going home.

THE LAST DRAGON
by **C.A. Rainfield**

*Book One of the
Dragon Speaker Series*

In the year 1144, dark times have fallen over the kingdom. Lord Manning rules through fear and magic, and the only hope seems to lie in the prophecy.

The prophecy says that a Dragon Speaker will appear to save the kingdom. Yet there are no dragons and no one who knows how to speak to them . . . except, perhaps, Jacob of Malden. Jacob is an unlikely hero — a small young man who walks with a limp and has the power to speak with birds.

But when the last dragon returns, it is only Jacob who can speak with her. It is only Jacob who can call upon her help. And ultimately it is Jacob — with his friends Orson and Lia — who rescues the egg holding the world's last male dragon.

ISBN 978-1-897039-46-5

www.hip-books.com/fantasy

A teacher's guide is available to cover all three novels.

A HERO'S WORTH
by **D.M. Ouellet**

*Book Two of the
Dragon Speaker Series*

Jacob and Orson must prove their worth in the battle against Lord Manning. Just as the baby dragon begins to grow, Lia is taken prisoner by her own father and will soon be forced to marry Lord Manning.

Jacob and Orson vow to rescue her. Orson manages to enter the castle to compete at the Samain Festival. He lets Jacob inside and the two combine to take on Lord Manning and his wizard, Kain. The battle is violent, with terrible injuries to both sides. Near the end, Kain is reaching into Jacob's mouth to extract a tooth – to add to his trophies – when there is a noisy surprise.

ISBN 978-1-897039-47-2

www.hip-books.com/fantasy

A teacher's guide is available to cover all three novels.

About the Author

E.L. Thomas spent much of her childhood with her nose buried in a book, and was sometimes late to school because of it. From Tolkien to Rowling, she's read about every dragon and elf in the many worlds of fantasy. For more information, see her website: www.erinthomas.ca

For more information on HIP novels:
High Interest Publishing
www.hip-books.com
391 Wellesley St. E. Toronto, Ontario M4X 1H5
2495 Main St. #452 Buffalo, New York 14214